DATE DUE			

Dedicated to the largely unsung, mostly unseen workers
for young people in need — L.H.
For Geordie — G.R.

Text copyright © 1994 by Libby Hathorn

Illustrations copyright © 1994 by Gregory Rogers

Published in 1994 in the United States of America by Crown Publishers, Inc.,
a Random House company, 201 East 50th Street, New York, New York 10022.
Originally published in Australia in 1994 by Random House Australia.

CROWN is a trademark of Crown Publishers, Inc.

Book design by Gregory Rogers

Manufactured in Hong Kong

Library of Congress Cataloging-in-Publication Data

Hathorn, Elizabeth.

Way home / by Libby Hathorn ; illustrated by Gregory Rogers. —

1st American ed.

p. cm.

Summary: Shane finds a no-name stray cat and takes it through the dangers of
the city to his home, a corner of an alley.

[1. Cats—Fiction. 2. Homeless persons—Fiction. 3. Home—Fiction. 4.

Friendship—Fiction.] I. Rogers, Gregory, ill. II. Title.

PZ7.H2843Way   1994   [Fic]—dc20   93-48030

ISBN 0-517-59909-0

10 9 8 7 6 5 4 3 2 1   First Edition

Way Home

by Libby Hathorn

illustrated by Gregory Rogers

Crown Publishers, Inc., New York

A dog barks and this cat with no name scrambles up a fence.

This boy called Shane sees the little cat and yells,

"Hey, you! Scaredy-cat!"

The cat with no name hears the loud voice of the boy.
And way up there on the top of the fence, this clever baby
thing rolls itself up. Such a tight little ball of fierce cat.
It growls and then it spits right at the boy called Shane.
Mad as anything!

"Heeey, wild cat! Wildcat!" the boy called Shane laughs.

"Heeey, I like you, Spitfire, Kitten Number One!"

He reaches out slowly, slowly to the ball of spiked fur.

"Sure I do. I like you.

And you like me, don't you?"

The boy called Shane strokes the scared fur.

He talks and talks until growls slide into silence.

"Guess what, Bestcat? You're coming home with me to my place."

And he lifts the cat with no name from the top of the fence.

He puts it deep inside his zip-up coat.

"Whadda you reckon, Catlegs?

Shane's taking you home right now."

Over the bins and garbage bags, past a row of seamed-up houses.

"Yeah — you're with me now, Cat. You 'n' me, Cat.

And we're going way away home . . . ."

But under a pool of streetlight the boy stops..

"Take a look at that Fatcat, will you? I'm telling you that cat's a loser. Eats fancy, no kidding. Right there at the window. Disgusting. And get that collar. What a joke!

"C'mon, Mycat, let's get lost."

The cat with no name is cozy inside the jacket against the
heartbeat of the boy called Shane.

"We're going home," the boy sings. "You 'n' me together."

The cat peers out of the warm boy's warm coat and purrs.

But halfway down the alley the boy stops dead.

"Here's a real nasty sight, Animal! Better belieeeve me.

That bunch down there, they don't like me.

"Don't panic now, Catlegs. Act kinda cool. Cool, right. That's us."

The boy called Shane glances back.

"Uh-oh, they're coming. Gotta get out of here. Away from them."

He pushes the little catface right down into his jacket.

And he runs hard. But they run hard too.

It's very black down there for the cat in the coat. There's a loud thump and a hard knock and a thud, thud, thud as the boy runs fast. They follow.

Go! Go! Down the alley, all the way they follow. Fast as anything, scared as anything. Go! Get away! Go! To a large lit-up street with the people going every which way. Right to an edge of a wide shiny river of cars.

"Hold tight, Kittycat, while I scare these guys."

The boy leaps out onto the avenue.

There's a blare of horns, a screaming of tongues and tires.

But the cat with no name feels safe in the boy's jacket.

"Ahhhh," the boy called Shane yells as he dives through

And all the way down the other side of the lit-up street the boy
is laughing and laughing. Past a showroom. Six shiny
sports cars, all in a row and one of them raised way up
high on a floor that's turning and turning.

"You can come out now, Whiskettes.
No worries. Hey, just take a look.
Vroom-vroom. You and me in a Jaguar. Vroom-vroom.
Huh, but they've only got red . . . and we want green."

Past busy windows and clean steps. Past a crumbling dark
church. Past the sharp smell of food shops. And the cat in

"Got yourself a cat, Shane?" a girl asks.

"I'm taking it home to my place," he tells her.

"Right now. Nonstop, express!"

"Bye, Shane," she calls after him.

But the boy called Shane stops again.

"See, they cook stuff right on the table in front of you.

Stacks of meat and things.

But don't get ideas, Hungry.

No pets allowed, places like this."

Past the light-and-stripe of the slatted shop blinds.

Past houses all lit up.

Past a thin forlorn park.

The boy called Shane peers down another long alley.

"No worries, Skinny Minny. Plenty of ways to go home.

And we're going this way.

But a dark shape comes bounding out of the long alley.
And the cat with no name sees a flash of cruel teeth,
hears the angry loud bark of the monster dog,
smells the blood and the hunger and danger.

Quick, in a panic, out of the coat, onto the fence, and into the
tree. Then up and up and up. The cat scritches and scratches
to the topmost, thinnest branches. It's hanging high in the
night city sky.

"Hey, Upcat — where you gone to, stupid?"
The boy called Shane, hand over hand, goes up and up
toward the topmost, thinnest branches.

"Forgot to tell you, Blackeyes, there's milk for you at home.
Lots and lots. So come here, okay?
We're friends. You said so.
C'mon, pussycat."

A steady brown hand reaches out. "I'd break my neck for you.
You know that? I'd break my stupid neck . . ."

The soft zippered jacket again and all the warmth against the chest of the boy called Shane.

"Sure, you can purr like mad now, Crazycat."

The boy called Shane, way up in the tree, stares over the

"Get that stack of big buildings.

Nobody lives in them — no way.

They're all mostly empty — 'specially nights.

I've been there once.

They're to look at, I guess.

So why don't you look, Kittycat?

Hey, get those people down there.

Talk about crazy.

There's our Jaguar too.

It's cool up here, I reckon."

"Guess what? I can see our place, Catseyes.

And we gotta go down right now."

Hand over hand, branch over branch, down the slippery trunk
to the tindery fence. It's an easy jump to the ground.

The boy called Shane takes the cat with no name back down.

"No more pussyfooting, Cat Number One. This time, we're
going right on home."

They go and go by buildings lit up and buildings in the dark,
until there's a path.
"Not far now.
Yeah. It's spooky right here. But we got each other, right?
Tread light, Shane boy. Real light."
The boy looks up and looks down. Then he crawls quickly,
quickly through a hole in a fence.

"From here on it's okay as anything, Noname.
No dogs, I promise. No fights.
And milk like I told you. Heaps of it.
Hang on now, we're nearly home.

"Down there and round here and we're almost — hey,
hold on real tight a minute,
through here and yes, yes! This is it, Mycat!

"This is my place.
Just like I said.
It's okay now.
You're safe.

"Here we are.
We're home!"